This book belongs to:

_____

Contents

Cover illustration and illustrations on pages 32-33 by Peter Stevenson

Published by Ladybird Books Ltd
27 Wrights Lane London W8 5TZ
A Penguin Company
5 7 9 10 8 6

Printed in Italy

Mystery
tour

written by Shirley Jackson
illustrated by Peter Stevenson

Let's go up the road,

up the hill and

down the hill and

round the trees and

over the river and

under the bridge...

to the funfair!

Put that back!

written by Lorraine Horsley
illustrated by Andrew Warrington

Can I have some sweets?

Can I have
a comic?

Can I have an
ice cream?

Hey!
That's cheating!

written by Marie Birkinshaw
illustrated by Graham Round

One for me and

one for you.

Two for me and

one for you.

Three for me and

one for you.

Wheels

written by Marie Birkinshaw
illustrated by David Parkins

One wheel,

two wheels,

three wheels,

four.

Four wheels?

Two wheels!

Four wheels no more!

New words introduced in this book

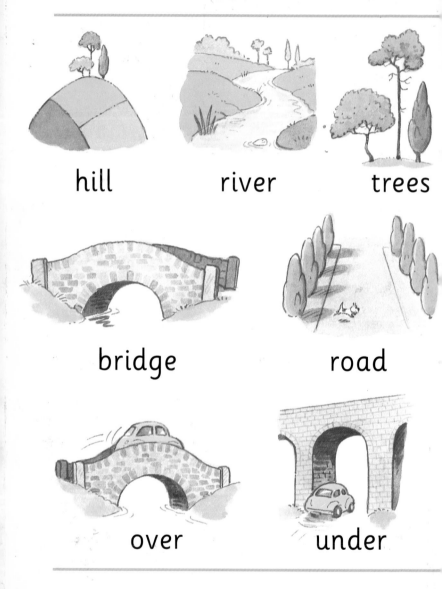

hill

river

trees

bridge

road

over

under

can, cheating, have, hey,